CLASSIC

Raggedy Ann & Andy

The Christmas Kitten

By Andrew Clements • Illustrated by Simon Galkin

LITTLE SIMON

New York   London   Toronto   Sydney   Singapore

 LITTLE SIMON

An imprint of Simon & Schuster Children's Publishing Division

1230 Avenue of the Americas

New York, New York 10020

Text and illustrations copyright © 2000 by Simon & Schuster, Inc. Cover illustration by Alison Winfield.

The names and depictions of Raggedy Ann and Raggedy Andy are trademarks of Simon & Schuster, Inc.

All rights reserved including the right of reproduction in whole or in part in any form.

LITTLE SIMON and colophon are registered trademarks of Simon & Schuster.

Manufactured in the United States of America

2 4 6 8 10 9 7 5 3

ISBN 0-689-83243-5

The dolls heard Marcella playing outside, and they ran to look down from the nursery window. After the big snowstorm, the world outside was white and crisp and clean.

"Doesn't that look like fun?" Raggedy Ann asked. "Soon Marcella will be flying down the hill by the Deep Deep Woods. This is a perfect Day Before Christmas!"

"I'm glad Marcella is having fun," said Raggedy Andy, "but I would like to go sledding too!"

"Ay, Laddy," said Uncle Clem. "Sliding down a hill is the best way there is to spend a winter's day!"

Raggedy Ann sat down and said, "I am going to think about something, and it would help if everyone could be quiet for a minute or two."

All her friends gathered around. Something special always happened whenever Raggedy Ann did some thinking.

After a few minutes, Raggedy Ann stood up. She announced, "I have an idea!"

The other dolls clapped their hands and shouted, "Hurrah! An idea! Raggedy Ann has got an idea!"

Raggedy Ann said, "Let's try some sledding ourselves! Who would like to go?"

Right away Raggedy Andy, Little Brown Bear, Uncle Clem, and Frederika raised their hands.

"Bravo!" cried Uncle Clem. "A Christmas Eve adventure!"

After dinner Marcella came to the nursery. She hugged each one of the dolls and then sat down with Raggedy Ann and Andy in her lap. She told them, "I went sledding today, and down I went like a whirly-swirly hurricane! Someday I shall take all of you for a ride. But now it's time for bed. In the morning you can come downstairs and see what Santa Claus has brought."

Then Marcella kissed all her dollies good night and hurried off to bed.

When the whole house was quiet, the dolls slipped out of the nursery and down the stairs.

One after another the dollies went out of Fido's flippy-flappy puppy door.

Raggedy Ann said, "I hope Marcella will not mind it if we borrow her sled."

"I'm sure it will be all right," said Raggedy Andy. "We will bring the sled right back as good as new!"

The moon shone brightly over the dolls when they climbed the hill.
Uncle Clem sat at the front of the sled, and the others got on behind him.
Just before she started pushing the sled, Raggedy Ann said, "Now, hold on tight!"

The sled went speeding down the hill like a shooting star.

Raggedy Andy yelled, "Hurray!"

The sled went faster and faster, and Raggedy Ann could see where they were headed—right toward a rushing brook!

Raggedy Ann said, "Uncle Clem, put your feet down!" Uncle Clem stuck his feet into the snow and—*wiffety, woffity, whoomp!*

The sled tipped over right at the edge of the brook, and dollies went flying every which way!

Little Brown Bear said, "My, oh, my! That was great! Let's go up and do it again!"

But just then Frederika put her fingers to her lips.

Raggedy Andy said, "I heard a sound coming from over there."

They followed the sound of a sad little cry.

Inside an old hollow log, they found a tiny kitten.

"There, there," said Raggedy Ann. "Don't cry, little kitty."

"Yes," said Raggedy Andy, "you will be safe and warm with us."

It was time to go, because taking care of a lost kitten was more important than taking another ride down the hill.

When they got back home, the dolls fed the kitty.

The kitty lapped up milk with his long pink tongue and licked the drops off his nose. Then he sat down, purr-purr-purring as he cleaned his face with his paws.

"Let's keep the kitty here as our pet!" said Raggedy Andy.

Frederika clapped her hands and said, "Yes! We can dress him up and take him for walks. The kitty can be like our own little dolly!"

Raggedy Ann got a dolly nightgown, and Frederika helped her put it on the kitty. They tucked him into a little bed by the window. Then everyone came to kiss the kitty good night.

When Raggedy Ann bent over to kiss him, some of her nice yarn hair fluttered down. One of the little kitty's paws shot out, and he tried to catch her hair.

"Oh!" cried Raggedy Ann.

The kitty scrambled out of the cradle, and quick as a wink, he pulled off the nightgown. Then he began chasing his tail and jumping at shadows in the moonlight.

Raggedy Ann sat down. "I am going to think about something," she announced.

Little Brown Bear whispered, "Shh. Raggedy Ann is thinking."

Everyone was quiet—all except the kitty.

After a few minutes, Raggedy Ann announced, "I have an idea! Now listen carefully—here's what we can do. . . ."

Everyone gathered around and listened to Raggedy Ann's idea.

Soon the nursery was bustling. There was a lot to do, because it was almost Christmas morning.

Bright and early on Christmas Day, Marcella took her dollies downstairs. When all the dolls were arranged on the couch, they could see that Santa Claus had not forgotten about Marcella!

Before long the packages were opened, and everyone was very happy. Then Mama said, "Look—back behind the Christmas tree. Is that another present?"

Marcella read the tag. "It says, 'For Marcella, with love from Santa Claus!' What could it be?"

Marcella lifted off the lid, and inside there was—nothing!

"It's empty! Has Santa played a joke on me?" Marcella asked.

Raggedy Ann almost fell off the couch! Where was that kitty? Was he lost again?

Just then there was a rustle in the branches of the Christmas tree.
Marcella looked up and saw two little yellow eyes staring out at her.

"Look!" she whispered. "It's a kitten! May I keep him, Daddy? May I, Mama?"

"Santa must have decided that this kitty needs a home," said Mama.

"Of course you may keep him!" said Daddy.

Marcella gently reached into the branches and picked up the kitten. She said, "I think his name should be Winky. Raggedy Ann, I'd like you and Raggedy Andy to meet our new friend, Winky. Winky, these are my dollies."

When Marcella put Winky on the couch with the dolls, he walked right

over to Raggedy Ann. He lay down in her lap and reached up to bat at her red yarn hair with his little black paws.

Marcella clapped her hands and laughed. "Look! Winky loves Raggedy Ann just like I do!"

And on that happy Christmas morning, Raggedy Ann knew for sure that being loved is the best feeling in the world.